Wilkie Collins

The Girl at the Gate

Good Press 2022

Wilkie Collins

The Girl at the Gate

Published by Good Press, 2022

goodpress@okpublishing.info

ISBN 978-80-272-2956-7

Contents

First Epoch.

TheItalians are born actors.

At this conclusion I arrived, flitting in a Roman theatre-now many years since. My friend and travelling companion, Rothsay, cordially agreed with me. Experience had given us some claim to form an opinion. We had visited, at that time, nearly every city in Italy. Wherever a theatre was open, we had attended the performances of the companies which travel from place to place; and we had never seen bad acting from first to last. Men and women, whose names are absolutely unknown in England, played (in modern comedy and drama for the most part) with a general level of dramatic ability which I have never seen equalled in the theatres of other nations. Incapable Italian actors there must be, no doubt. For my own part I have only discovered them, by ones and twos, in England; appearing among the persons engaged to support Salvini and Ristori before the audiences of London.

On the occasion of which I am now writing, the night's performances consisted of two plays. An accident, to be presently related, prevented us from seeing more than the introductory part of the second piece. That one act-in respect of the influence which the remembrance of it afterwards exercised over Rothsay and myself-claims a place of its own in the opening pages of the present narrative.

The scene of the story was laid in one of the principalities of Italy, in the byegone days of the Carbonaro conspiracies. The chief persons were two young noblemen, friends affectionately attached to each other, and a beautiful girl born in the lower ranks of life.

On the rising of the curtain, the scene before us was the courtyard of a prison. We found the beautiful girl (called Celia as well as I can recollect) in great distress; confiding her sorrows to the gaoler's daughter. Her father was pining in the prison, charged with an offence of which he was innocent; and she herself was suffering the tortures of hopeless love. She was on the point of confiding her secret to her friend, when the appearance of the young noblemen closed her Ops. The girls at once withdrew; and the two friends-whom I now only remember as The Marquis and The Count-began the dialogue which prepared us for the story of the play.

The Marquis has been tried for conspiracy against the reigning Prince and his government; has been found guilty, and is condemned to be shot that evening. He accepts his sentence with the resignation of a man who is weary of his life. Young as he is, he has tried the round of pleasures without enjoyment; he has no interests, no aspirations, no hopes; he looks on death as a welcome release. His friend the Count, admitted to a farewell interview, has invented a stratagem by which the prisoner may escape and take to flight. The Marquis expresses a grateful sense of obligation, and prefers being shot. "I don't value my life," he says; "I am not a happy man like you." Upon this the Count mentions circumstances which he has hitherto kept secret. He loves the charming Celia, and loves in vain. Her reputation is unsullied; she possesses every good quality that a man can desire in a wife-but the Count's social position forbids him to marry a woman of low birth. He is heartbroken; and he too finds life without hope a burden that is not to be borne. The Marquis at once sees a way of devoting himself to his friend's interests. He is rich; his money is at his own disposal; he will bequeath a marriage portion to Celia which will make her one of the richest women in Italy. The Count receives this proposal with a sigh. "No money," he says, "will remove the obstacle that still remains. My father's fatal objection to Celia is her rank in life." The Marquis walks apart-considers a little-consults his watch-and returns with a new idea. "I have nearly two hours of life still left," he says. "Send for Celia: she was here just now, and she is probably in her father's cell." The Count is at a loss to understand what this proposal means. The Marquis explains himself. "I ask your permission," he resumes, "to offer marriage to Celia-for your sake. The chaplain of the prison will perform the ceremony. Before dark, the girl you love will be my widow. My widow is a lady of title —a fit wife for the greatest nobleman in the land." The Count protests and refuses in vain. The gaoler is sent to find Celia. She appears. Unable to endure the scene, the Count rushes out in horror. The Marquis makes his offer of marriage, and excuses it by appealing to the girl's love for her father.

If she becomes a lady of rank, she will be in a position to procure the liberty of the innocent old man, whose strength is fast failing him under the rigours of imprisonment. Celia hesitates. After a struggle with herself, filial love prevails, and she consents. The gaoler announces that the chaplain is waiting; the bride and bridegroom withdraw to the prison chapel. Left on the stage, the gaoler hears a distant sound in the city, which he is at a loss to understand. It sinks, increases again, travels nearer to the prison, and now betrays itself as the sound of multitudinous voices in a state of furious uproar. Has the conspiracy broken out again? Yes! The whole population has risen; the soldiers have refused to fire on the people; the terrified Prince has dismissed his ministers, and promises a constitution. The Marquis, returning from the ceremony which has just made Celia his wife, is presented with a free pardon, and with the offer of a high place in the reformed ministry. A new life is opening before him-and he has innocently ruined his friend's prospects! On this striking situation the drop-curtain falls.

While we were still applauding the first act, Rothsay alarmed me: he dropped from his seat at my side, like a man struck dead. The stifling heat in the theatre had proved too much for him. We carried him out at once into the fresh air. When he came to his senses, my friend entreated me to leave him, and see the end of the play. To my mind, he looked as if he might faint again. I insisted on going back with him to our hotel.

On the next day I went to the theatre, to ascertain if the play would be repeated. The box-office was closed. The dramatic company had left Rome.

My interest in discovering how the story ended led me next to the booksellers' shops-in the hope of buying the play. Nobody knew anything about it. Nobody could tell me whether it was the original work of an Italian writer, or whether it had been stolen (and probably disfigured) from the French. As a fragment I had seen it. As a fragment it has remained, from that time to this.

Second Epoch.

One of my objects in writing these lines is to vindicate the character of an innocent woman (formerly in my service as house-keeper) who has been cruelly slandered. Absorbed in the pursuit of my purpose, it has only now occurred to me that strangers may desire to know something more than they know now of myself and my friend. "Give us some idea," they may say, "of what sort of persons you are, if you wish to interest us at the outset of your story." A most reasonable suggestion, I admit. Unfortunately, I am not the right person to comply with it.

In the first place, I cannot pretend to pronounce judgment on my own character. In the second place, I am incapable of writing impartially of my friend. At the imminent risk of his own life, Rothsay rescued me from a dreadful death by accident, when we were at college together. Who can expect me to speak of his faults? I am not even capable of seeing them.

Under these embarrassing circumstances-and not forgetting, at the same time, that a servant's opinion of his master and his master's friends may generally be trusted not to err on the favourable side —I am tempted to call my valet as a witness to character.

I slept badly on our first night at Rome; and I happened to be awake while the man was talking of us confidentially in the courtyard of the hotel-just under my bedroom window. Here, to the best of my recollection, is a faithful report of what he said to some friend among the servants who understood English: —

"My master's well connected, you must know-though he's only plain Mr. Lepel. His uncle's the great lawyer, Lord Lepel; and his late father was a banker. Rich, did you say? I should think he *was* rich-and be hanged to him! No; not married, and not likely to be. Owns he was forty last birthday; a regular old bachelor. Not a bad sort, taking him altogether. The worst of him is, he is one of the most indiscreet persons I ever met with. Does the queerest things, when the whim takes him, and doesn't care what other people think of it. They say the Lepels have all got a slate loose in the upper story. Oh, no; not a very old family —I mean nothing compared to the family of his friend, young Rothsay. *They* count back, as I have heard, to the ancient Kings of Scotland. Between ourselves, the ancient Kings haven't left the Rothsays much money. They would be glad, I'll be bound, to get my rich master for one of their daughters. Poor as Job, I tell you. This young fellow travelling with us has never had a spare five pound note since he was born. Plenty of brains in his head, I grant you; and a little too apt sometimes to be suspicious of other people. But liberal-oh, give him his due-liberal in a small way. Tips me with a sovereign now and then. I take it-Lord bless you, I take it. What do you say? Has he got any employment? Not he! Dabbles in chemistry (experiments and that sort of thing) by way of amusing himself; and tells the most infernal lies about it. The other day he showed me a bottle about as big as a thimble, with what looked like water in it, and said it was enough to poison everybody in the hotel What rot! Isn't that the clock striking again) Near about bedtime, I should say. Wish you good night."

There are our characters-drawn on the principle of justice without mercy, by an impudent rascal who is the best valet in England. Now you know what sort of persons we are; and now we may go on again.

Rothsay and I parted, soon after our night at the theatre. He went to Civita Vecchia to join a friend's yacht, waiting for him in the harbour. I turned homeward, travelling at a leisurely rate through the Tyrol and Germany.

After my arrival in England, certain events in my life occurred, which did not appear to have any connection at the time. They led nevertheless to consequences which seriously altered the relations of happy past years between Rothsay and myself.

The first event took place on my return to my house in London. I found among the letters waiting for me, an invitation from Lord Lepel to spend a few weeks with him at his country seat in Sussex.

I had made so many excuses, in past years, when I received invitations from my uncle, that I was really ashamed to plead engagements in London again. There was no unfriendly feeling between us. My only motive for keeping away from him took its rise in dislike of the ordinary modes of life in an English country house. A man who feels no interest in politics, who cares nothing for field sports, who is impatient of amateur music and incapable of small talk, is a man out of his element in country society. This was my unlucky case. I went to Lord Lepel's house sorely against my will; longing already for the day when it would he time to say goodbye.

The routine of my uncle's establishment had remained unaltered since my last experience of it.

I found my lord expressing the same pride in his collection of old masters, and telling the same story of the wonderful escape of his picture-gallery from fire —I renewed my acquaintance with the same members of parliament among the guests, all on the same side in politics —I joined in the same dreary amusements —I saluted the same resident priest (the Lepels are all born and bred Roman Catholics) —I submitted to the same rigidly early breakfast hour; and inwardly cursed the same peremptory bell, ringing as a means of reminding us of our meals. The one change that presented itself was a change out of the house. Death had removed the lodge-keeper at the park gate. His widow and daughter (Mrs. Rymer and little Susan) remained in their pretty cottage. They had been allowed by my lord's kindness to take charge of the gate.

Out walking, on the morning after my arrival, I was caught in a shower on my way back to the park, and took shelter in the lodge.

In the byegone days, I had respected Mrs. Rymer's husband as a thoroughly worthy man-but Mrs. Rymer herself was no great favourite of mine. She had married beneath her, as the phrase is, and she was a little too conscious of it. A woman with a sharp eye to her own interests; selfishly discontented with her position in life, and not very scrupulous in her choice of means when she had an end in view: that is how I describe Mrs. Rymer. Her daughter, whom I only remembered as a weakly child, astonished me when I saw her again after the interval that had elapsed. The backward flower had bloomed into perfect health. Susan was now a lovely little modest girl of seventeen-with a natural delicacy and refinement of manner, which marked her to my mind as one of Nature's gentlewomen. When I entered the lodge she was writing at a table in a comer, having some books on it, and rose to withdraw. I begged that she would proceed with her employment, and asked if I might know what it was. She answered me with a blush, and a pretty brightening of her clear blue eyes. "I am trying, sir, to teach myself French," she said. The weather showed no signs of improving —I volunteered to help her, and found her such an attentive and intelligent pupil that I looked in at the lodge from time to time afterwards, and continued my instructions. The younger men among my uncle's guests set their own stupid construction on my attentions to "the girl at the gate," as they called her-rather too familiarly, according to my notions of propriety. I contrived to remind them that I was old enough to be Susan's father, in a manner which put an end to their jokes; and I was pleased to hear, when I next went to the lodge, that Mrs. Rymer had been wise enough to keep these facetious gentlemen at their proper distance.

The day of my departure arrived. Lord Lepel took leave of me kindly, and asked for news of Rothsay. "Let me know when your friend returns," my uncle said; "he belongs to a good old stock. Put me in mind of him when I next invite you to come to my house."

On my way to the train I stopped of course at the lodge to say goodbye. Mrs. Rymer came out alone. I asked for Susan.

"My daughter is not very well to-day."

"Is she confined to her room?"

"She is in the parlour."

I might have been mistaken, but I thought Mrs. Rymer answered me in no very friendly way. Resolved to judge for myself I entered the lodge, and found my poor little pupil sitting in a corner, crying. When I asked her what was the matter, the excuse of a "bad headache" was the only reply that I received. The natures of young girls are a hopeless puzzle to me. Susan seemed, for some reason which it was impossible to understand, to be afraid to look at me. "Have you and your mother been quarrelling?" I asked.

"Oh, no!"

She denied it with such evident sincerity that I could not for a moment suspect her of deceiving me. Whatever the cause of her distress might be, it was plain that she had her own reasons for keeping it a secret.

Her French books were on the table. I tried a little allusion to her lessons. "I hope you will go on regularly with your studies," I said.

"I will do my best, sir-without you to help me."

She said it so sadly that I proposed-purely from the wish to encourage her—a continuation of our lessons through the post. "Send an exercise to me once a week," I suggested; "and I will return it corrected,"

She thanked me in low tones, with a shyness of manner which I had never noticed in her before. I had done my best to cheer her-and I was conscious, as we shook hands at parting, that I had failed. A feeling of disappointment overcomes me when I see young people out of spirits. I was sorry for Susan.

Third Epoch.

ONE of my faults (which has not been included in the list set forth by my valet) is a disinclination to occupy myself with my own domestic affairs. The proceedings of my footman, while I had been away from home, left me no alternative but to dismiss him on my return. With this exertion of authority my interference as chief of the household came to an end. I left it to my excellent housekeeper, Mrs. Mozeen, to find a sober successor to the drunken vagabond who had been sent away. She discovered a respectable young man-tall, plump, and rosy-whose name was Joseph, and whose character was beyond reproach. I have but one excuse for noticing such a trifling event as this. It took its place, at a later period, in the chain which was slowly winding round me.

My uncle had asked me to prolong my visit; and I should probably have consented, but for anxiety on the subject of a near and dear relative-my sister. Her health had been failing since the death of her husband, to whom she was tenderly attached. I heard news of her while I was in Sussex, which hurried me back to town. In a month more, her death deprived me of my last living relation. She left no children; and my two brothers had both died unmarried while they were still young men.

This affliction placed me in a position of serious embarrassment, in regard to the disposal of my property after my death.

I had hitherto made no will; being well aware that my fortune (which was entirely in money) would go in due course of law to the person of all others who would employ it to the best purpose-that is to say, to my sister as my nearest of kin. As I was now situated, my property would revert to my uncle if I died intestate. He was a richer man than I was. Of his two children, both sons, the eldest would inherit his estates: the youngest had already succeeded to his mother's ample fortune. Having literally no family claims on me, I felt bound to recognise the wider demands of poverty and misfortune, and to devote my superfluous wealth to increasing the revenues of charitable institutions. As to minor legacies, I owed it to my good housekeeper, Mrs. Mozeen, not to forget the faithful services of past years. Need I add-if I had been free to act as I pleased-that I should have gladly made Rothsay the object of a handsome bequest? But this was not to be. My friend was a man morbidly sensitive on the subject of money. . In the early days of our intercourse, we had been for the first and only time on the verge of a quarrel, when I had asked (as a favour to myself) to be allowed to provide for him in my will.

"It is because I am poor," he explained, "that I refuse to profit by your kindness-though I feel it gratefully."

I failed to understand him-and said so plainly.

"You will understand this," he resumed; "I should never recover my sense of degradation, if a mercenary motive on my side was associated with our friendship. Don't say it's impossible! You know as well as I do that appearances would be against me, in the eyes of the world. Besides, I don't want money; my own small income is enough for me. Make me your executor if you like, and leave me the customary present of five hundred pounds. If you exceed that sum, I declare on my word of honour that I will not touch one farthing of it." He took my hand, and pressed it fervently. "Do me a favour," he said. "Never let us speak of this again!"

I understood that I must yield-or lose my friend.

In now making my will, I accordingly appointed Rothsay one of my executors, on the terms that he had prescribed. The minor legacies having been next duly reduced to writing, I left the bulk of my fortune to public charities.

My lawyer laid the fair copy of the will on my table. "A dreary disposition of property for a man of your age," he said. "I hope to receive a new set of instructions before you are a year older."

"What instructions?" I asked.

"To provide for your wife and children," he answered.

My wife and children! The idea seemed to be so absurd that I burst out laughing. It never occurred to me that there could be any absurdity in my own point of view.

I was sitting alone, after my legal adviser had taken his leave, looking absently at the newly-engrossed will, when I heard a sharp knock at the house door which I thought I recognised. In another minute Rothsay's bright face enlivened my dull room. He had returned from the Mediterranean that morning.

"Am I interrupting you?" he asked, pointing to the leaves of manuscript before me. "Are you writing a book?"

"I am making my will."

His manner changed; he looked at me seriously. "Do you remember what I said, when we once talked of your will?" he asked. I set his doubts at rest immediately-but he was not quite satisfied yet. "Can't you put your will away?" he suggested. "I hate the sight of anything that reminds me of death."

"Give me a minute to sign it," I said-and rang to summon the witnesses.

Mrs. Mozeen answered the bell. Rothsay looked at her, as if he wished to have my housekeeper put away as well as my will. From the first moment when he had seen her, he conceived a great dislike to that good creature. There was nothing, I am sure, personally repellent about her. She was a little slim quiet woman, with a pale complexion and bright brown eyes. Her movements were gentle; her voice was low; her decent grey dress was adapted to her age. Why Rothsay should dislike her was more than he could explain himself. He turned his unreasonable prejudice into a joke-and said he hated a woman who wore slate-coloured cap-ribbons! I explained to Mrs. Mozeen that I wanted witnesses to the signature of my will. Naturally enough-being in the room at the time-she asked if she could be one of them.

I was obliged to say No; and, not to mortify her, I gave the reason. "My will recognises what I owe to your good services," I said. "If you are one of the witnesses, you will lose your legacy. Send up the men-servants."

With her customary tact, Mrs. Mozeen expressed her gratitude silently, by a look-and left the room.

"Why couldn't you tell that woman to send the servants, without mentioning her legacy?" Rothsay asked. "My friend Lepel, you have done a very foolish thing."

"In what way?"

"You have given Mrs. Mozeen an interest in your death."

It was impossible to make a serious reply to this ridiculous exhibition of Rothsay's prejudice against poor Mrs. Mozeen.

"When am I to be murdered?" I asked. "And how is it to be done? Poison?"

"I'm not joking," Rothsay answered. "You are infatuated about your housekeeper. When you spoke of her legacy, did you notice her eyes?"

"Yes."

"Did nothing strike you?"

"It struck me that they were unusually well preserved eyes for a woman of her age."

The appearance of the valet and the footman put an end to this idle talk. The will was executed, and locked up. Our conversation turned on Rothsay's travels by sea. The cruise had been in every way successful. The matchless shores of the Mediterranean defied description; the sailing of the famous yacht had proved to be worthy of her reputation; and, to crown all, Rothsay had come back to England in a fair way, for the first time in his life, of making money.

"I have discovered a treasure," he announced.

"What is it?"

"It *was* a dirty little modern picture, picked up in a bye-street at Palermo. It *is* a Virgin and Child, by Guido."

On further explanation, it appeared that the picture exposed for sale was painted on copper. Noticing the contrast between the rare material and the wretchedly bad painting that covered it, Rothsay had called to mind some of the well-known stories of valuable works of art that had been painted over for purposes of disguise. The price asked for the picture amounted to little more than the value of the metal. Rothsay bought it. His knowledge of chemistry enabled him to put his suspicion successfully to the test; and one of the guests on board the yacht —a famous French artist-had declared his conviction that the picture now revealed to view was a genuine work by Guido. Such an opinion as this convinced me that it would be worth while to submit my friend's discovery to the judgment of other experts. Consulted independently, these critics confirmed the view taken by the celebrated personage who had first seen the work. This result having been obtained, Rothsay asked my advice next on the question of selling his picture. I at once thought of my uncle. An undoubted work by Guido would surely be an acquisition to his gallery. I had only (in accordance with his own request) to let him know that my friend had returned to England. We might take the picture with us, when we received our invitation to Lord Lepel's house.

Fourth Epoch.

My uncle's answer arrived by return of post. Other engagements obliged him to defer receiving us for a month. At the end of that time, we were cordially invited to visit him, and to stay as long as we liked.

In the interval that now passed, other events occurred-still of the trifling kind.

One afternoon, just as I was thinking of taking my customary ride in the Park, the servant appeared charged with a basket of flowers, and with a message from Mrs. Rymer, requesting me to honour her by accepting a little offering from her daughter. Hearing that she was then waiting in the hall, I told the man to show her in. Susan (as I ought to have already mentioned) had sent her exercises to me regularly every week. In returning them corrected, I had once or twice added a word of well-deserved approval. The offering of flowers was evidently intended to express my pupil's grateful sense of the interest taken in her by her teacher.

I had no reason, this time, to suppose that Mrs. Rymer entertained an unfriendly feeling towards me. At the first words of greeting that passed between us I perceived a change in her manner, which ran into the opposite extreme. She overwhelmed me with the most elaborate demonstrations of politeness and respect; dwelling on her gratitude for my kindness in receiving her, and on her pride at seeing her daughter's flowers on my table, until I made a resolute effort to stop her by asking (as if it was actually a matter of importance to me!) whether she was in London on business or on pleasure.

"Oh, on business, sir! My poor husband invested his little savings in bank stock, and I have just been drawing my dividend. I do hope you don't think my girl over-bold in venturing to send you a few flowers. She wouldn't allow me to interfere. I do assure you she would gather and arrange them with her own hands. In themselves I know they are hardly worth accepting; but if you will allow the motive to plead — —"

I made another effort to stop Mrs. Rymer; I said her daughter could not have sent me a prettier present.

The inexhaustible woman only went on more fluently than ever. "She is so grateful, sir, and so proud of your goodness in looking at her exercises. The difficulties of the French language seem as nothing to her, now her motive is to please you. She is so devoted to her studies that I find it difficult to induce her to take the exercise necessary to her health; and, as you may perhaps remember, Susan was always rather weakly as a child. She inherits her father's constitution, Mr. Lepel-not mine."

Here, to my infinite relief, the servant appeared, announcing that my horse was at the door.

Mrs. Rymer opened her mouth. I saw a coming flood of apologies on the point of pouring out-and seized my hat on the spot. I declared I had an appointment; I sent kind remembrances to Susan (pitying her for having such a mother with my whole heart); I said I hoped to return to my uncle's house soon, and to continue the French lessons. The one thing more that I remember was finding myself safe in the saddle, and out of the reach of Mrs. Rymer's tongue.

Reflecting on what had passed, it was plain to me that this woman had some private end in view, and that my abrupt departure had prevented her from finding the way to it. What motive could she possibly have for that obstinate persistence in presenting poor Susan under a favourable aspect, to a man who had already shown that he was honestly interested in her pretty modest daughter? I tried hard to penetrate the mystery-and gave it up in despair.

Three days before the date at which Rothsay and I were to pay our visit to Lord Lepel, I found myself compelled to undergo one of the minor miseries of human life. In other words, I became one of the guests at a large dinner party. It was a rainy day in October. My position at the table placed me between a window that was open, and a door that was hardly ever shut. I went to bed, shivering; and woke the next morning with a headache and a difficulty in breathing. On consulting the doctor, I found that I was suffering from an attack of bronchitis. There was no reason to be alarmed. If I remained indoors, and submitted to the necessary treatment, I might hope to keep my engagement with my uncle in ten days or a fortnight.

There was no alternative but to submit. I accordingly arranged with Rothsay that he should present himself at Lord Lepel's house (taking the picture with him), on the date appointed for our visit, and that I should follow as soon as I was well enough to travel.

On the day when he was to leave London, my friend kindly came to keep me company as usual. He was followed into my room by Mrs. Mozeen, with a bottle of medicine in her hand. This worthy creature, finding that the doctor's directions occasionally escaped my memory, devoted herself to the duty of administering the remedies at the prescribed intervals of time. When she left the room, having performed her duties as usual, I saw Rothsay's eyes follow her to the door with an expression of sardonic curiosity. He put a strange question to me as soon as we were alone.

"Who engaged that new servant of yours?" he asked. "I mean the fat fellow, with the curly, flaxen hair."

"Hiring servants," I replied, "is not much in my way. I left the engagement of the new man to Mrs. Mozeen."

Rothsay walked gravely up to my bedside. "Lepel," he said, "your respectable housekeeper is in love with the fat young footman."

It is not easy to amuse a man suffering from bronchitis. But this new outbreak of absurdity was more than I could resist, even with a mustard plaster on my chest.

"I thought I should raise your spirits," Rothsay proceeded "When I came to your house this morning, the valet opened the door to me. I expressed my surprise at his condescending to take that trouble. He informed me that Joseph was otherwise engaged. 'With anybody in particular?' I asked, humouring the joke. 'Yes, sir, with the housekeeper. She's teaching him how to brush his hair, so as to show off his good looks to the best advantage.' Make up your mind, my friend, to lose Mrs. Mozeen-especially if she happens to have any money."

"Nonsense, Rothsay! The poor woman is old enough to be Joseph's mother."

"My good fellow, that won't make any difference to Joseph. In the days when we were rich enough to keep a manservant, our footman-as handsome a fellow as ever you saw, and no older than I am-married a witch with a lame leg. When I asked him why he had made such a fool of himself he looked quite indignant, and said, 'Sir! she has got six hundred pounds.' He and the witch keep a public-house. What will you bet me that we don't see your housekeeper drawing beer at the bar, and Joseph getting drunk in the parlour, before we are a year older."

I was not well enough to prolong my enjoyment of Rothsay's boyish humour. Besides, exaggeration to be really amusing must have some relation, no matter how slender it may be, to the truth. My housekeeper belonged to a respectable family, and was essentially a person accustomed to respect herself. Her brother occupied a position of responsibility in the establishment of a firm of chemists whom I had employed for years past. Her late husband had farmed his own land, and had owed his ruin to calamities for which he was in no way responsible. Kind-hearted Mrs. Mozeen was just the woman to take a motherly interest in a well-disposed lad like Joseph; and it was equally characteristic of my valet-especially when Rothsay was thoughtless enough to encourage him-to pervert an innocent action for the sake of indulging in a stupid jest. I took advantage of my privilege as an invalid and changed the subject.

A week passed. I had expected to hear from Rothsay. To my surprise and disappointment no letter arrived.

Susan was more considerate. She wrote, very modestly and prettily, to say that she and her mother had heard of my illness from Mr. Rothsay, and to express the hope that I should soon be restored to health. A few days later, Mrs. Rymer's politeness carried her to the length of taking the journey to London, to make inquiries at my door. I did not see her, of course. She left word that she would have the honour of calling again.

The second week followed. I had by that time, perfectly recovered from my attack of bronchitis-and yet I was too ill to leave the house.

The doctor himself seemed to be at a loss to understand the symptoms that now presented themselves. A vile sensation of nausea tried my endurance, and an incomprehensible prostration of strength depressed my spirits. I felt such a strange reluctance to exert myself, that I actually left it to Mrs. Mozeen to write to my uncle in my name, and say that I was not yet well enough to visit him. My medical adviser tried various methods of treatment; my housekeeper administered the prescribed medicines with unremitting care; but nothing came of it. A physician of great authority was called into consultation. Being completely puzzled, he retreated to the last refuge of bewildered doctors. I asked him what was the matter with me. And he answered, "Suppressed gout."

Fifth Epoch.

MIDWAY in the third week, my uncle wrote to me as follows: —

"I have been obliged to request your friend Rothsay to bring his visit to a conclusion. Although he refuses to confess it, I have reason to believe that he has committed the folly of falling seriously in love with the young girl at my lodge gate. I have tried remonstrance in vain; and I write to his father at the same time that I write to you. There is much more that I might say. I reserve it for the time when I hope to have the pleasure of seeing you restored to health."

Two days after the receipt of this alarming letter, Rothsay returned to me.

Ill as I was, I forgot my sufferings the moment I looked at him. Wild and haggard, he stared at me with bloodshot eyes like a man demented.

"Do you think I am mad? I daresay I am. I can't live without her." Those were the first words he said when we shook hands.

But I had more influence over him than any other person; and, weak as I was, I exerted it. Little by little, he became more reasonable; he began to speak like his old self again.

To have expressed any surprise, on my part, at what had happened would have been not only imprudent, but unworthy of him and of me. My first inquiry was suggested by the fear that he might have been hurried into openly confessing his passion to Susan-although his position forbade him to offer marriage. I had done him an injustice. His honourable nature had shrunk from the cruelty of raising hopes, which, for all he knew to the contrary, might never be realised. At the same time, he had his reasons for believing that he was at least personally acceptable to her. "She was always glad to see me," said poor Rothsay. "We constantly talked of you. She spoke of your kindness so prettily and so gratefully. Oh, Lepel, it is not her beauty only that has won my heart! Her nature is the nature of an angel." His voice failed him. For the first time in my remembrance of our long companionship, he burst into tears.

I was so shocked and distressed that I had the greatest difficulty in preserving my own self-control. In the effort to comfort him, I asked if he had ventured to confide in his father. "You are the favourite son," I reminded him. "Is there no gleam of hope in the future?"

He had written to his father. In silence he gave me the reply.

It was expressed with a moderation which I had hardly dared to expect. Mr. Rothsay the elder admitted that he had himself married for love, and that his wife's rank in the social scale (although higher than Susan's) had not been equal to his own. "In such a family as ours," he wrote-perhaps with pardonable pride —"we raise our wives to our own degree. But this young person labours under a double disadvantage. She is obscure, and she is poor. What have you to offer her? Nothing. And what have I to give you? Nothing."

This meant, as I interpreted it, that the main obstacle in the way was Susan's poverty. And I was rich! In the excitement that possessed me, I followed the impulse of the moment headlong, like a child.

"While you were away from me," I said to Rothsay, "did you never once think of your old friend? Must I remind you that I can make Susan your wife with one stroke of my pen?" He looked at me in silent surprise. I took my cheque-book from the drawer of the table, and placed the inkstand within reach. "Susan's marriage portion," I said, "is a matter of a line of writing, with my name at the end of it."

He burst out with an exclamation that stopped me, just as my pen touched the paper. "Good heavens," he cried, "you are thinking of that play we saw at Rome! Are we on the stage? Are you performing the part of the Marquis-and am I the Count?"

I was so startled by this wild allusion to the past —I recognised with such astonishment the reproduction of the dramatic situation in the play, at a crisis in his life and mine-that the use of the pen remained suspended in my hand. For the first time in my life, I was conscious of a sensation of superstitious dread.

Rothsay recovered himself first. He misinterpreted what was passing in my mind.

"Don't think me ungrateful," he said. "You dear kind good fellow, consider for a moment, and you will see that it can't be. What would be said of her and of me, if you made Susan rich with your money, and if I married her? The poor innocent would be called your cast-off mistress. People would say, 'He has behaved liberally to her, and his needy friend has taken advantage of it.'"

The point of view which I had failed to see was put with such terrible directness of expression, that the conviction that I was wrong was literally forced on me. What reply could I make? Rothsay evidently felt for me. "You are ill," he said gently; "let me leave you to rest." He held out his hand to say good-bye. I insisted on his taking up his abode with me, for the present at least. Ordinary persuasion failed to induce him to yield. I put it on selfish grounds next "You have noticed that I am ill," I said, "I want you to keep me company." He gave way directly.

Through the wakeful night, I tried to consider what moral remedies might be within our reach. The one useful conclusion at which I could arrive was to induce Rothsay to try what absence and change might do to compose his mind. To advise him to travel alone was out of the question. I wrote to his one other old friend besides myself-the friend who had taken him on a cruise in the Mediterranean.

The owner of the yacht had that very day given directions to have his vessel laid up for the winter season. He at once countermanded the order by telegraph. "I am an idle man," he said, "and I am as fond of Rothsay as you are. I will take him wherever he likes to go." It was not easy to persuade the object of these kind intentions to profit by them. Nothing that I could say roused him. I spoke to him of his picture. He had left it at my uncle's house, and neither knew nor cared to know whether it had been sold or not. The one consideration which ultimately influenced Rothsay was presented by the doctor; speaking as follows (to quote his own explanation) in the interests of my health: —

"I warned your friend, Mr. Lepel, that his conduct was causing anxiety which you were not strong enough to bear. On hearing this he at once promised to follow the advice which you had given to him, and to join the yacht. As you know, he has kept his word. May I ask if he has ever followed the medical profession?"

Replying in the negative, I begged the doctor to tell me why he had put his question.

He answered, "Mr. Rothsay requested me to tell him all that I knew about your illness. I complied of course; mentioning that I had lately adopted a new method of treatment, and that I had every reason to feel confident of the results. He was so interested in the symptoms of your illness, and in the remedies being tried, that he took notes in his pocketbook of what I had said. When he paid me that compliment, I thought it possible that I might be speaking to a colleague."

I was pleased to hear of my friend's anxiety for my recovery. If I had been in better health, I might have asked myself what reason he could have had for making those entries in his pocketbook.

Three days later another proof reached me of Rothsay's anxiety for my welfare.

The owner of the yacht wrote to beg that I would send him a report of my health, addressed to a port on the south coast of England, to which they were then bound. "If we don't hear good news," he added, "I have reason to fear that Rothsay will overthrow our plans for the recovery of his peace of mind by leaving the vessel, and making his own inquiries at your bedside."

With no small difficulty, I roused myself sufficiently to write a few words with my own hand. They were words that lied-for my poor friend's sake. In a postscript, I begged my correspondent to let me hear if the effect produced on Rothsay had answered to our hopes and expectations.

(*To be Continued.*)

Sixth Epoch

THE weary days followed each other-and time failed to justify the doctor's confidence in his new remedies, I grew weaker and weaker. My uncle came to see me. He was so alarmed that he insisted on a consultation being held with hie own physician. Another great authority was called in, at the same time, by the urgent request of my own medical man. These distinguished persons held more than one privy council, before they would consent to give a positive opinion. It was an evasive opinion (encumbered with hard words of Greek and Roman origin) when it was at last pronounced. I waited until they had taken their leave, and then appealed to my own doctor. "What do those men really think?" I asked. "Shall I live, or die?"

The doctor answered for himself as well as for his illustrious colleagues. "We have great faith in the new prescriptions," he said.

I understood what that meant. They were afraid to tell me the truth. I insisted on the truth.

"How long shall I live?" I said. "Till the end of the year?"

The reply followed in one terrible word: "Perhaps."

It was then the first week in December. I understood that I might reckon-at the utmost-on three weeks of life. What I felt, on arriving at this conclusion, I shall not say. It is the one secret I keep from the readers of these lines.

The next day Mrs. Rymer called once more to make inquiries. Not satisfied with the servant's report, she entreated that I would consent to see her. My housekeeper, with her customary kindness, undertook to convey the message. If she had been a wicked woman, would she have acted in this way? "Mrs. Rymer seems to be sadly distressed," she pleaded. "As I understand, sir, she is suffering under some domestic anxiety which can only be mentioned to yourself."

Did this anxiety relate to Susan? The bare doubt of it decided me. I consented to see Mrs. Rymer. Feeling it necessary to control her in the use of her tongue, I spoke the moment the door was opened.

"I am suffering from illness; and I must ask you to spare me as much as possible. What do you wish to say to me?"

The tone in which I addressed Mrs. Rymer would have offended a more sensitive woman. The truth is, she had chosen an unfortunate time for her visit. There were fluctuations in the progress of my malady; there were days when I felt better, and days when I felt worse-and this was a bad day. Moreover, my uncle had tried my temper that morning. He had called to see me, on his way to winter in the south of France by his physician's advice; and he recommended a trial of change of air in my case also. His country house (only thirty miles from London) was entirely at my disposal; and the railway supplied beds for invalids. It was useless to answer that I was not equal to the effort. He reminded me that I had exerted myself to leave my bedchamber for my arm-chair in the next room, and that a little additional resolution would enable me to follow his advice. We parted in a state of irritation on either side which, so far as I was concerned, had not subsided yet.

"I wish to speak to you, sir, about my daughter," Mrs. Rymer answered. The mere allusion to Susan had its composing effect on me. I said kindly that I hoped she was well.

"Well in body," Mrs. Rymer announced. "Far from it, sir, in mind."

Before I could ask what this meant, we were interrupted by the appearance of the servant, bringing the letters which had arrived for me by the afternoon post. I told the man, impatiently, to put them on the table at my side.

"What is distressing Susan?" I inquired, without stopping to look at the letters.

"She is fretting, sir, about your illness. Oh, Mr. Lepel, if you would only try the sweet country air! If you only had my good little Susan to nurse you!"

She too taking my uncle's view! And talking of Susan as my nurse!

"What are you thinking of?" I asked her. "A young girl like your daughter nursing Me! You ought to have more regard for Susan's good name?"

"I know what *you* ought to do!" She made that strange reply with a furtive look at me; half in anger, half in alarm.

"Go on," I said.

"Will you turn me out of your house for my impudence?" she asked.

"I will hear what you have to say to me. What ought I to do?"

"Marry Susan."

I heard the woman plainly-and yet, I declare I doubted the evidence of my senses.

"She's breaking her heart for you," Mrs. Rymer burst out. "She's been in love with you, since you first darkened our doors-and it will end in the neighbours finding it out. I did my duty to her; I tried to stop it; I tried to prevent you from seeing her, when you went away. Too late; the mischief was done. When I see my girl fading day by day-crying about you in secret, talking about you in her dreams —I can't stand it; I must speak out. Oh, yes, I know how far beneath you she is-the daughter of your uncle's servant. But she's your equal, sir, in the sight of Heaven. My lord's priest converted her only last year-and my Susan is as good a Papist as yourself."

How could I let this go on? I felt that I ought to have stopped it before.

"It's possible," I said, "that you may not be deliberately deceiving me. If you are yourself deceived, I am bound to tell you the truth. Mr. Rothsay loves your daughter, and, what is more, Mr. Rothsay has reason to know that Susan — —"

"That Susan loves him?" she interposed, with a mocking laugh. "Oh, Mr. Lepel, is it possible that a clever man like you can't see clearer than that? My girl in love with Mr. Rothsay! She wouldn't have looked at him a second time if he hadn't talked to her about you. When I complained privately to my lord of Mr. Rothsay hanging about the lodge, do you think she turned as pale as ashes, and cried when *he* passed through the gate, and said goodbye?"

She had complained of Rothsay to Lord Lepel —I understood her at last! She knew that my friend and all his family were poor. She had put her own construction on the innocent interest that I had taken in her daughter. Careless of the difference in rank, blind to the malady that was killing me, she was now bent on separating Rothsay and Susan, by throwing the girl into the arms of a rich husband like myself!

"You are wasting your breath," I told her; "I don't believe one word you say to me."

"Believe Susan, then!" cried the reckless woman. "Let me bring her here. If she's too shamefaced to own the truth, look at her-that's all I ask-look at her, and judge for yourself!"

This was intolerable. In justice to Susan, in justice to Rothsay, I insisted on silence.

"No more of it?" I said. "Take care how you provoke me. Don't you see that I am ill? don't you see that you are irritating me to no purpose?"

She altered her tone. "I'll wait," she said quietly, "while you compose yourself."

With those words, she walked to the window, and stood there with her back towards me. Was the wretch taking advantage of my helpless condition? I stretched out my hand to ring the bell, and have her sent away-and hesitated to degrade Susan's mother, for Susan's sake. In my state of prostration, how could I arrive at a decision? My mind was dreadfully disturbed; I felt that the first necessity was to find some means of tranquillising myself. Looking about me, the letters on the table attracted my attention. Mechanically, I took them up; mechanically, I put them down again. Two of them slipped from my trembling fingers: my eyes fell on the uppermost of the two. The address was in the handwriting of the good friend with whom Rothsay was sailing.

Just as I had been speaking of Rothsay here was the news of him for which I had asked!

I opened the letter and read these words:

"There is, I fear, but little hope for our friend-unless this girl on whom he has set his heart can (by some lucky change of circumstances) become his wife. He has tried to master his weakness; but his own infatuation is too much for him. He is really and truly in a state of despair. Two evenings since-to give you a melancholy example of what I mean —I was in my cabin, when I heard the alarm of a man overboard. The man was Rothsay. My sailing-master, seeing that he was unable to swim, jumped into the sea and rescued him, as I got on deck.

Rothsay declares it to have been an accident; and everybody believes him but myself. I know the state of his mind. Don't be alarmed; I will have him well looked after; and I won't give him up just yet. We are still bound southward, with a fair wind. If the new scenes which I hope to show him prove to be of no avail, I must reluctantly take him back to England. In that case, which I don't like to contemplate, you may see him again-perhaps in a month's time."

He might return in a month's time-return to hear that he had lost the one friend, on whose power and will to help him he might have relied. If I failed to employ in his interests the short interval of life still left to me, could I doubt (after what I just read) what the end would be? How could I help him? Oh, God! how could I help him?

Mrs. Rymer left the window, and returned to the chair which she had occupied when I first received her.

"Are you quieter in your mind now?" she asked.

I neither answered her nor looked at her.

Still determined to reach her end, she tried again to force her unhappy daughter on me. "Will you consent," she persisted, "to see Susan?"

If she had been a little nearer to me, I am afraid I should have struck her. "You wretch!" I said, "do you know that I am a dying man?"

"While there's life there's hope," Mrs. Rymer remarked.

I ought to have controlled myself; but it was not to be done.

"Hope of your daughter being my rich widow?" I asked.

Her bitter answer followed instantly.

"Even then," she said, "Susan wouldn't marry Rothsay."

I looked at her—I repeated the words after her: "Susan wouldn't marry Rothsay."

The thought burst on my mind, like light bursting on the eyes of a man restored to sight. If Susan agreed to go through the form of marriage with a dying bridegroom, my rich widow could (and would) become Rothsay's wife. Once more, the remembrance of the play at Rome returned, and set the last embers of resolution which sickness and suffering had left to me in a flame. The devoted friend of that imaginary story had counted on death to complete his generous purpose in vain: *he* had been condemned by the tribunal of man, and had been reprieved. I—in his place, and with his self-sacrifice in my mind-might found a firmer trust in the future; for I had been condemned by the tribunal of God.

Encouraged by my silence, the obstinate woman persisted. "Won't you even send a message to Susan?" she asked.

Rashly, madly, without an instant's hesitation, I answered:

"Go back to Susan, and say I leave it to *her*."

Mrs. Rymer started to her feet. "You leave it to Susan to be your wife, if she likes?"

"I do."

"And if she consents?"

"*I* consent,"

In two weeks and a day from that time, the deed was done. When Rothsay returned to England, he would ask for Susan-and he would find my virgin-widow rich and free.

Seventh Epoch.

Whatever may be thought of my conduct, let me say this in justice to myself—I was resolved that Susan should not be deceived.

Half an hour after Mrs. Rymer bad left my house, I wrote to her daughter, plainly revealing the motive which led me to offer marriage, solely in the future interest of Rothsay and herself. "If you refuse," I said, in conclusion, "you may depend on my understanding you and feeling for you. But, if you consent-then I have a favour to ask. Never let us speak to one another of the profanation that we have agreed to commit, for your faithful lover's sake."

I had formed a high opinion of Susan-too high an opinion as it seemed. Her reply surprised and disappointed me. In other words, she gave her consent.

I stipulated that the marriage should be kept strictly secret, for a certain period. In my own mind I decided that the interval should be held to expire, either on the day of my death, or on the day when Rothsay returned.

My next proceeding was to write in confidence to the priest whom I have already mentioned, in an earlier part of these pages. He has reasons of his own for not permitting me to disclose the motive which induced him to celebrate my marriage privately in the chapel at Lord Lepel's house. My uncle's desire that I should try change of air, as offering a last chance of recovery, was known to my medical attendant, and served as a sufficient reason (although he protested against the risk) for my removal to the country. I was carried to the station, and placed on a bed-slung by ropes to the ceiling of a saloon carriage, so as to prevent me from feeling the vibration when the train was in motion. Faithful Mrs. Mozeen entreated to be allowed to accompany me. I was reluctantly compelled to refuse compliance with this request, in justice to the claims of my lord's housekeeper; who had been accustomed to exercise undivided authority in the household, and who had made every preparation for my comfort. With her own hands, Mrs. Mozeen packed everything that I required, including the medicines prescribed for the occasion. She was deeply affected, poor soul, when we parted.

I bore the journey-happily for me it was a short one-better than had been anticipated. For the first few days that followed, the purer air of the country seemed, in some degree, to revive me. But the deadly sense of weakness, the slow sinking of the vital power in me, returned as the time drew near for the marriage. The ceremony was performed at night. Only Susan and her mother were present. No persons in the house but ourselves had the faintest suspicion of what had happened.

I signed my new will (the priest and Mrs. Rymer being the witnesses) in my bed that night. It left everything that I possessed, excepting a legacy to Mrs. Mozeen, to my wife.

Obliged, it is needless to say, to preserve appearances, Susan remained at the lodge as usual. But it was impossible to resist her entreaty to be allowed to attend on me, for a few hours daily, as assistant to the regular nurse. When she was alone with me, and had no inquisitive eyes to dread, the poor girl shewed a depth of feeling, which I was unable to reconcile with the motives that could alone have induced her (as I then supposed) to consent to the mockery of our marriage. On occasions when I was so far able to resist the languor that oppressed me as to observe what was passing at my bedside—I saw Susan look at me, as if there were thoughts in her pressing for utterance which she hesitated to express. Once, she herself acknowledged this. "I have so much to say to you," she owned, "when you are stronger and fitter to hear me." At other times, her nerves seemed to be shaken by the spectacle of my sufferings. Her kind hands trembled and made mistakes, when they had any nursing duties to perform near me. The servants noticing her, used to say, "That pretty girl seems to be the most awkward person in the house." On the day that followed the ceremony in the chapel, this want of self-control brought about an accident which led to serious results.

In removing the small chest which held my medicines from the shelf on which it was placed, Susan let it drop on the floor. The two full bottles still left were so completely shattered that not even a tea-spoonful of the contents was saved.

Shocked at what she had done, the poor girl volunteered to go herself to my chemist in London, by the first train. I refused to allow it. What did it matter to me now, if my death from exhaustion was hastened by a day or two? Why need my life be prolonged artificially by drugs when I had nothing left to live for? An excuse for me which would satisfy others was easily found. I said that I had been long weary of physic, and that the accident had decided me on refusing to take more.

That night I did not wake quite so often as usual. When she came to me the next day, Susan noticed that I looked better. The day after, the other nurse made the same observation. At the end of the week, I was able to leave my bed, and sit by the fireside, while Susan read to me. Some mysterious change in my health had completely falsified the prediction of the medical men. I sent to London for my doctor-and told him that the improvement in me had begun on the day when I left off taking my remedies. "Can you explain it?" I asked. He answered that no such "resurrection from the dead" (as he called it) had ever happened in his long experience. On leaving me, he asked for the latest prescriptions that had been written. 1 inquired what he was going to do with them. "I mean to go to the chemist," he replied, "and to satisfy myself that your medicines have been properly made up."

I owed it to Mrs. Mozeen's true interest in me, to tell her what had happened. The same day I wrote to her. I also mentioned what the doctor had said, and asked her to call on him, and ascertain if the prescriptions had been shown to the chemist, and if any mistake had been made.

A more innocently intended letter than this never was written. And yet there are people who have declared that it was inspired by suspicion of Mrs. Mozeen!

Eighth Epoch.

WHETHER I was so weakened by illness as to be incapable of giving my mind to more than one subject for reflection at a time (that subject being now the extraordinary recovery of my health) —or whether I was pre-occupied by the effort, which I was in honour bound to make, to resist the growing attraction to me of Susan's society—I cannot presume to say. This only I know: when the discovery of the terrible position towards Rothsay in which I now stood, suddenly overwhelmed me, an interval of some days had passed. I cannot account for it. I can only say-so it was.

Susan was in the room. I was wholly unable to hide from her the sudden change of colour which betrayed the horror that had overpowered me. She said anxiously, "What has frightened you?"

I don't think I heard her. The play was in my memory again-the fatal play, which had wound itself into the texture of Rothsay's life and mine. In vivid remembrance, I saw once more the dramatic situation of the first act, and shrank from the reflection of it in the disaster which had fallen on my friend and myself.

"What has frightened you?" Susan repeated.

I answered in one word—I whispered his name: "Rothsay!"

She looked at me in innocent surprise. "Has he met with some misfortune?" she asked quietly.

"Misfortune"—did she call it? Had I not said enough to disturb her tranquillity in mentioning Rothsay's name? "I am living!" I said. "Living-and likely to live!"

Her answer expressed fervent gratitude "Thank God for it?"

I looked at her, astonished as she had been astonished when she looked at me.

"Susan, Susan," I cried—"must I own it? I love you!"

She came nearer to me with timid pleasure in her eyes-with the first faint light of a smile playing round her lips.

"You say it very strangely," she murmured. "Surely, my dear one, you ought to love me? Since the first day when you gave me my French lesson—havn't I loved You?"

"*You* love *me?*" I repeated. "Have you read — —?" My voice failed me; I could say no more.

She turned pale. "Read-what?" she asked.

"My letter."

"What letter?"

"The letter I wrote to you before we were married."

Am I a coward? The bare recollection of what followed that reply makes me tremble. Time has passed. I am a new man now; my health is restored; my happiness is assured: I ought to be able to write on. No: it is not to be done. Does the man live, who in my place could record the suffering that I innocently, most innocently, inflicted on the sweetest and truest of women? Nothing saved us from a parting as absolute as the parting that follows death, but the confession that had been wrung from me at a time when my motive spoke for itself. The artless avowal of her affection had been justified, had been honoured, by the words which laid my heart at her feet when I said "I love you."

••••

She had risen to leave me. In a last look, we had silently resigned ourselves to wait, apart from each other, for the day of reckoning that must follow Rothsay's return-when we heard the sound of carriage-wheels on the drive that led to the house. In a minute more, the man himself entered the room.

He looked first at Susan-then at me. In both of us he saw the traces that told of agitation endured, but not yet composed. Worn and weary he waited, hesitating, near the door.

"Am I intruding?" he asked.

"We were thinking of you, and speaking of you," I replied, "just before you came in."

"*We?*" he repeated, turning towards Susan once more. After a pause, he offered me his hand-and drew it back.

"You don't shake hands with me," he said.

"I am waiting, Rothsay, until I know that we are the same firm friends as ever."

For the third time he looked at Susan. "Will *you* shake hands?" he asked.

She gave him her hand cordially. "May I stay here?" she said, addressing herself to me.

In my situation at that moment, I understood the generous purpose that animated her. But she had suffered enough already—I led her gently to the door. "It will be better," I whispered, "if you will wait down stairs in the library." She hesitated. "What will they say in the house?" she objected, thinking of the servants, and of the humble position which she was still supposed to occupy. "It matters nothing what they say, now," I told her. She left us.

"There seems to be some private understanding between you," Rothsay said, when we were alone.

"You shall hear what it is," I answered. "But I must beg you to excuse me if I speak first of myself."

"Are you alluding to your health?"

"Yes."

"Quite needless, Lepel. I met your doctor this morning. I know that a council of physicians decided you would die before the year was out."

He paused there.

"And they proved to be wrong," I added.

"They might have proved to be right," Rothsay rejoined, "but for the accident which spilt your medicine, and the despair of yourself which decided you on taking no more."

I could hardly believe that I understood him. "Do you assert," I said, "that my medicine would have killed me, if I had taken the rest of it?"

"I have no doubt that it would."

"Will you explain what you mean?"

"Let me have your explanation first. I was not prepared to find Susan in your room. I was surprised to see traces of tears in her face. Something has happened in my absence. Am I concerned in it?"

"You are."

I said it quietly-in full possession of myself. The trial of fortitude through which I had already passed seemed to have blunted my customary sense of feeling. I approached the disclosure which I was now bound to make with steady resolution, resigned to the worst that could happen when the truth was known.

"Do you remember the time," I resumed, "when I was so eager to serve you that I proposed to make Susan your wife by making her rich?"

"Yes."

"Do you remember asking me if I was thinking of the play we saw together at Rome? Is the story as present to your mind now, as it was then?"

"Quite as present."

"You asked if I was performing the part of the Marquis-and if you were the Count. Rothsay! the devotion of that ideal character to his friend has been *my* devotion; his conviction that his death would justify what he had done for his friend's sake, has been *my* conviction; and as it ended with him, so it has ended with me-his terrible position is *my* terrible position towards you, at this moment."

"Are you mad?" Rothsay asked sternly.

I passed over that first outbreak of his anger in silence.

"Do you mean to tell me you have married Susan?" he went on.

"Bear this in mind," I said. "When I married her, I was doomed to death. Nay more. In your interests-as God is my witness—I welcomed death."

He stepped up to me, in silence, and raised his hand with a threatening gesture. That action at once deprived me of my self-possession. I spoke with the ungovernable rashness of a boy.

"Carry out your intention," I said. "Insult me."

His hand dropped.

"Insult me," I repeated; "it is one way out of the unendurable situation in which we are placed. You may trust me to challenge you. Duels are still fought on the Continent; I will follow you abroad; I will choose pistols; I will take care that we fight on the fatal foreign system; and I will purposely miss you. Make her what I intended her to be-my rich widow."

He looked at me attentively.

"Is *that* your refuge?" he asked, scornfully. "No! I won't help you to commit suicide."

God forgive me! I was possessed by a spirit of reckless despair; I did my best to provoke him.

"Reconsider your decision," I said; "and remember-you tried to commit suicide yourself."

He turned quickly to the door, as if he distrusted his own powers of self-control.

"I wish to speak to Susan," he said, keeping his back turned on me.

"You will find her in the library."

He left me.

I went to the window. I opened it, and let the cold wintry air blow over my burning head. I don't know how long I sat at the window. There came a time when I saw Rothsay on the house steps. He walked rapidly towards the park gate. His head was down; he never once looked back at the room in which he had left me.

As he passed out of my sight, I felt a hand laid gently on my shoulder. Susan had returned to me.

"He will not come back," she said. "Try still to remember him as your old friend. He asks you to forgive and forget."

She had made the peace between us. I was deeply touched; my eyes filled with tears as I looked at her. She kissed me on the forehead, and went out. I afterwards asked what had passed between them when Rothsay spoke with her in the library. She never has told me what they said to each other; and she never will. She is right.

Later in the day, I was told that Mrs. Rymer had called, and wished to "pay her respects."

I refused to see her. Whatever claim she might have otherwise had on my consideration had been forfeited by the infamy of her conduct, when she intercepted my letter to Susan. Her sense of injury, on receiving my message, was expressed in writing, and was sent to me the same evening. The last sentence in her letter was characteristic of the woman.

"However your pride may despise me," she wrote, "I am indebted to you for the rise in life that I have always desired. You may refuse to see me-but you can't prevent my being the mother-in-law of a gentleman."

Soon afterwards, I received a visit which I had hardly ventured to expect. Busy as he was in London, my doctor came to see me. He was not in his usual good spirits.

"I hope you don't bring me any bad news," I said.

"You shall judge for yourself," he replied. "I come from Mr. Rothsay, to say for him what he in not able to say for himself."

"Where is he?"

"He has left England."

"For any purpose that you know of?"

"Yes. He has sailed to join the expedition of rescue—I ought rather to call it the forlorn hope-which is to search for the lost explorers in Central Australia."

In other words, he had gone to seek death in the fatal footsteps of Burke and Wills. I could not trust myself to speak.

The doctor saw that there was a reason for my silence, and that he would do well not to notice it. He changed the subject.

"May I ask," he said, "if you have heard from the servants left in charge at your house in London?"

"Has anything happened?"

"Something has happened which they are evidently afraid to tell you; knowing the high opinion which you have of Mrs. Mozeen. She has suddenly quitted your service, and has gone, nobody knows where. I have taken charge of a letter which she left for you."

He handed me the letter. As soon as I had recovered myself, I looked at it.

There was this inscription on the address: —"For my good master, to wait until he returns home."

The few lines in the letter itself ran thus: —"Distressing circumstances oblige me to leave you, sir, and do not permit me to enter into particulars. In asking your pardon, I offer my sincere thanks for your kindness, and my fervent prayers for your welfare."

That was all. The date had a special interest for me. Mrs. Mozeen had written on the day when she must have received my letter-the letter which has already appeared in these pages.

"Is there really nothing known of the poor woman's motives?" I asked.

"There are two explanations suggested," the doctor informed me. "One of them, which is offered by your female servants, seems to me absurd. They declare that Mrs. Mozeen, at her mature age, was in love with the young man who is your footman! It is even asserted that she tried to recommend herself to him, by speaking of the money which she expected to bring to the man who would make her his wife. The footman's reply, informing her that he was already engaged to be married, is alleged to be the cause which has driven her from your house."

I begged that the doctor would not trouble himself to repeat more of what my women servants had said. "If the other explanation," I added, "is equally unworthy of notice — —"

"The other explanation," the doctor interposed, "comes from Mr. Rothsay, and is of a very serious kind."

Rothsay's opinion demanded my respect. "What view does he take?" I inquired.

"A view that startles me," the doctor said. "You remember my telling you of the interest he took in your symptoms, and in the remedies I had employed? Well! Mr. Rothsay accounts for the incomprehensible recovery of your health, by asserting that poison-probably administered in small quantities, and intermitted at intervals in fear of discovery-has been mixed with your medicine; and he asserts that the guilty person is Mrs. Mozeen."

It was impossible that I could openly express the indignation that I felt on hearing this. My position towards Rothsay forced me to restrain myself.

"May I ask," the doctor continued, "if Mrs. Mozeen was aware that she had a legacy to expect at your death?"

"Certainly."

"Has she a brother who is one of the dispensers employed by your chemists?"

"Yes."

"Did she know that I doubted if my prescriptions had been properly prepared, and that I intended to make inquiries?"

"I wrote to her myself on the subject."

"Do you think her brother told her that I was referred to *him*, when I went to the chemists?"

"I have no means of knowing what her brother did."

"Can you at least tell me when she received your letter?"

"She must have received it on the day when she left my house."

The doctor rose with a grave face. "These are rather extraordinary coincidences," he remarked.

I merely replied, "Mrs. Mozeen is as incapable of poisoning as I am."

The doctor wished me good morning.

I repeat here my conviction of my housekeeper's innocence. I protest against the cruelty which accuses her. And, whatever may have been her motive in suddenly leaving my service, I declare that she still possesses my sympathy and esteem, and I invite her to return to me if she ever sees these lines.

I have only to add, by way of postscript, that we have heard of the safe return of the expedition of rescue. Time, as my wife and I both hope, may yet convince Rothsay that he will not be wrong in counting on Susan's love-the love of a sister.

In the meanwhile, we possess a memorial of our absent friend. We have bought his picture.

THE END.

Printed in Great Britain
by Amazon

37893090R00022